Your Favourite
THOMAS THE TANK ENGINE
Story Collection

D1116335

DEAN

Stories first published in Great Britain 1990, 1991
by Buzz Books, an imprint of Reed Children's Books
Michelin House, 81 Fulham Road, London SW3 6RB
and Auckland, Melbourne, Singapore and Toronto
This edition published 1995 by Dean
in association with Heinemann Young Books
Copyright © William Heinemann Ltd 1990, 1991
All publishing rights William Heinemann Ltd
All television and merchandising rights
licensed by William Heinemann Limited to
Britt Allcroft (Thomas) Ltd, exclusively, worldwide
Photographs © Britt Allcroft (Thomas) Ltd 1985, 1986
Photographs by David Mitton, Kenny McArthur and
Terry Permane for Britt Allcroft's production of
Thomas the Tank Engine and Friends

ISBN 0 603 55423 7

Produced by Mandarin Offset Ltd
Printed and bound in China

Contents

Thomas and Terence

Autumn had come to the Island of Sodor. The leaves were changing from green to brown. The fields were changing too, from yellow stubble to brown earth.

As Thomas puffed along on his branch line with Annie and Clarabel, he heard the "chug chug chug" of a tractor at work.

One day, stopping for a signal, he saw the tractor close by.

"Hullo!" said the tractor. "I'm Terence; I'm ploughing."

"Hullo!" said Thomas. "I'm Thomas; I'm pulling a train. What *ugly* wheels you've got."

Terence said that his wheels were not ugly.

"They are caterpillars not wheels!" he said. "I can go anywhere; *I* don't need rails like you."

"I don't want to go *anywhere*," said Thomas, huffily. "I like my rails, thank you."

Soon winter came with dark heavy clouds, full of snow. Thomas's driver didn't like it.

"A heavy snow fall is coming," he said. "I do hope it doesn't stop us."

"Pooh!" said Thomas. "Snow is silly soft stuff, there's nothing to it!" And he puffed on, taking no notice.

Thomas finished his journey safely, but by now the fields were covered and the rails were two dark lines standing out in the white snow.

"You'll need your snow plough for the next journey, Thomas," said his driver.

"Pooh! Snow is silly soft stuff – it won't stop me!" Thomas snorted.

"Listen to me," said his driver. "We are going to put this snow plough on and I want no nonsense, please!"

The snow plough was heavy and uncomfortable and made Thomas cross. He shook it and banged it all day long and when they finally got back to the shed it was so damaged that the driver had to take it off.

"You're a very naughty engine and I am very cross with you!" the driver said, as he closed the shed door that night.

Next morning, Thomas's driver and fireman arrived earlier than usual. Even though they worked very hard to mend the snow plough, they were unable to fix it.

Soon it was time for the first train and Thomas was feeling very pleased with himself.

"I shan't have to wear it! I shan't have to wear it!" he puffed.

"I hope it's all right. I hope it's all right," Annie and Clarabel whispered to each other.

The driver was worried too.

"The snow's not bad here," he said to the fireman, "but it's sure to be deep in the valley."

It had been snowing again. Thomas started with his train full of passengers.

"Silly soft stuff! Silly soft stuff!" he puffed. "I didn't need that stupid old thing yesterday and I shan't need it today. Snow can't stop *me*."

Thomas rushed into the tunnel, thinking how clever he was. But there was trouble ahead.

At the other end of the tunnel he could see that a heap of snow had fallen from the sides of the cutting.

"Silly soft stuff!" said Thomas and he charged into the snow. "Cinders and ashes!" he cried. "I'm stuck!" – and he was.

"Back, Thomas, back!" called his driver.

Thomas tried to go back but his wheels spun round and round and he couldn't move.

"Oh, what shall I do?" cried Thomas. More snow fell down and piled up around him.

The guard went back for help while the driver, fireman and passengers tried to dig the snow from Thomas's wheels.

But as fast as they dug, more snow slipped down and Thomas was nearly buried.

"Oh! My wheels and coupling rods!" said Thomas. "I shall have to stop here until I'm completely frozen. Oh, what a silly engine I am." And Thomas began to cry.

At last a bus came to rescue all the passengers. Then Terence the tractor came chugging through the tunnel.

Snow never worried him.

He pulled the empty coaches away quickly and then came back for Thomas.

Terence pushed aside all the snow so that Thomas was no longer buried. Thomas's wheels were now clear but they still spun round and round when he tried to move. Terence tugged and slipped, and slipped and tugged.

At last he pulled Thomas clear of the snow, ready for the journey home.

"Thank you, Terence, your caterpillars are *splendid*," said Thomas, gratefully.

"I hope that you will be sensible now, Thomas," said his driver, crossly.

"I'll try," said Thomas, as he puffed his way home.

James and the Tar Wagons

Toby is a tram engine. He is short and sturdy and has a coach called Henrietta. They enjoy their job on the Island of Sodor.

Every morning they take the workmen to the quarry and they often meet James the red engine at the junction.

Toby and Henrietta look very old-fashioned.

When they first came they were shabby and needed new paint, and James was rude whenever he saw them.

"Ugh! What dirty objects!" he would say as they passed by.

One day Toby lost patience.

"James," he said, "why are you red?"

"I am a splendid engine," replied James, loftily. "I am ready for anything. You never see *my* paint dirty."

"Oh," said Toby, innocently, "that's why you once needed bootlaces – to be ready, I suppose!"

James felt redder than ever. He snorted off angrily down the line. It was such an insult to be reminded of the time when a passenger's bootlace had been used to mend a hole in one of his coaches.

And all because he had gone too fast.

At the end of the line James left his coaches and quickly got ready for his next train. It was a 'slow goods', stopping at every station to pick up and set down trucks. James hated slow goods trains.

"Dirty trucks from dirty sidings!" he grumbled. Starting with only a few, James picked up more and more trucks until he had a long train.

He was not at all happy.

At first, the trucks behaved well but James bumped them so crossly that they soon decided to pay him back.

They went over the viaduct and it wasn't long before they reached the top of Gordon's hill. Heavy goods trains should wait there so that the guard can 'pin down' their brakes. This stops the trucks pushing the engines too fast as they go down the hill.

James had had an accident with trucks once before on Gordon's hill. He should have remembered this.

"Wait, James, wait!" called his driver, but James was not listening.

He was too busy thinking about what he would say to Toby when they next met.

"Hurrah! Hurrah!" laughed the naughty trucks. They banged their buffers and pushed James hard down the hill. The guard tightened his brakes but it was no good.

"On! On! On! On!" cried the trucks.

"I've *got* to stop. I've *got* to stop," groaned James.

They thundered through the station and lurched into the yard.

There was an enormous crash and something sticky hit James.

He had run into two tar wagons and was black from smoke-box to cab. He was more dirty than hurt, but the wagons and some trucks were broken to pieces. The breakdown train was in the yard and they soon tidied up the mess.

Toby and Percy arrived to help.

"Look there, Percy!" said Toby. "Whatever is that dirty object?"

"That's James," replied Percy.

"Didn't you know?"

"Well, it's James's shape," said Toby, "but James is a splendid _red_ engine and you never see _his_ paint dirty."

James pretended that he hadn't heard.

Toby and Percy cleared away the unhurt trucks and helped James home. The Fat Controller came down to the yard to meet them.

"Well done, Percy and Toby!" he said, smiling.

He turned to James.

"Fancy letting your trucks run away. I *am* surprised! You're not fit to be seen; you must be cleaned at once, he said to the unhappy engine.

"Toby shall have a new coat of paint – chocolate and blue, I think," said the Fat Controller. "Please, sir, can Henrietta have one too?" asked Toby.

"Certainly, Toby," said the Fat Controller. "She shall have brown, like Annie and Clarabel, Thomas's coaches."

Toby smiled. He knew that Henrietta would be delighted and he ran off happily to tell her the good news.

Thomas, Percy and the Coal

It was a beautiful morning on the Island of Sodor. Thomas the Tank Engine's blue paint sparkled in the sunshine as he puffed happily along the branchline with his coaches, Annie and Clarabel.

Thomas made good time and soon arrived at the station where Toby and Percy were waiting. He was feeling very pleased with himself.

"Hello, Thomas!" whistled Percy. "You look splendid!"

"Yes, indeed," boasted Thomas. "Blue is the only proper colour for an engine."

"Oh, I don't know. I like my brown paint," said Toby.

"I've always been green. I wouldn't want to be any other colour either," added Percy.

"Well, anyway," huffed Thomas, "blue is the only colour for a Really Useful Engine – everyone knows that."

Percy said no more; he just grinned at Toby. They knew only too well that sometimes Thomas could be a little too cheeky for his own good.

Later, Thomas was resting in a siding when Percy arrived in the yard. Percy pulled his trucks to a large hopper to load them with coal.

Thomas was still being cheeky.

"Careful, Percy," he warned. "Watch out with those silly trucks."

"Go on! go on!" muttered the trucks as Percy pulled each one under the hopper.

"And by the way," Thomas went on, "those buffers don't look very safe to *me*. . ."

But he got no further. With a tremendous bump, the last truck passed the hopper much too fast. The coal poured down – all over Thomas.

"Help, I'm choking!" cried Thomas. "Get me out!"

Percy was worried, but he couldn't help laughing. Thomas's smart blue paint was covered in coal dust, from smoke-box to bunker.

"Ha! Ha!" chuckled Percy. "You don't look Really Useful now, Thomas. You look really disgraceful."

"I'm not disgraceful," choked Thomas. "You did that on purpose. Get me out!"

It took the men so long to clean Thomas that he wasn't in time for his next train. Toby had to take Annie and Clarabel instead.

"Poor Thomas," whispered Annie and Clarabel. They were most upset. Thomas was upset, too. He was very grumpy in the shed that night.

Toby thought it a great joke, but Percy was cross with Thomas for thinking that *he* had made Thomas's paint dirty on purpose.

"Fancy a Really Useful Blue engine like Thomas becoming a disgrace to the Fat Controller's railway!" said Percy. "Pooh! I wouldn't have missed all that fun for anything," he chuckled.

Thomas was at the platform the next day when Percy brought his trucks in from the junction. The trucks were heavy.

"I feel so tired," Percy puffed as he pulled into the station.

"Why don't you go off and have a drink," said his driver. "Then you'll feel better."

The water column stood at the end of the siding with the unsafe buffers. The props underneath the buffers were old and needed mending. Percy moved forward and found that he couldn't stop. The buffers didn't stop him either!

"Oooh," wailed Percy. "Somebody help me!"

The buffers were broken and Percy was wheel-deep in coal.

It was time for Thomas to leave. He had seen everything.

"Now Percy has learnt his lesson, too," he chuckled to himself.

That night the two engines made up their quarrel.

"I didn't cause your accident on purpose, Thomas," whispered Percy. "You do know that, don't you?"

"Of course," replied Thomas. "And I'm sorry I was cheeky. Your green paint looks splendid again, too. In future, we'll both be more careful of coal," said Thomas wisely.

Saved From Scrap

The Fat Controller works his engines hard but they are always very proud when he calls them Really Useful.

"I'm going to the scrapyard today," Edward called to Thomas.

"What, already? You're not that old!" replied Thomas cheekily.

The scrapyard is full of rusty old cars and machinery.

They are brought to the yard to be broken into pieces and loaded into trucks.

Then Edward pulls them to the steel works where they are melted down and used again.

One day, when Edward arrived in the yard, there was a surprise waiting for him. It was a traction engine.

"Hello," said Edward. "You're not broken and rusty. What are you doing here?"

"I'm Trevor," said the Traction Engine sadly. "They're going to break me up next week."

"What a shame!" said Edward.

"My driver says I only need some paint, polish and oil to be as good as new," Trevor went on sadly, "but my master says that I'm old-fashioned."

Edward snorted. "People say that *I'm* old-fashioned, but I don't care. The Fat Controller says that I'm a Useful Engine. What work did you do?" he asked.

"My master used to send us from farm to farm. We threshed corn, hauled logs and did lots of other work. We made friends at all the farms. The children loved to see us."

Trevor shut his eyes – remembering. "Oh yes," he replied, dreamily. "I like children."

Edward set off for the station.

"Broken up, what a shame! Broken up, what a shame!" he clanked as he went back to work. "I must help Trevor, I *must*."

He thought of all his friends who liked engines but strangely none of them would have room for a traction engine at home!

"It's a shame! It's a shame!" Edward hissed as he went over the viaduct.

Then he brought his coaches to the station.

"Peep, peep!" he whistled. "Why didn't I think of him before?" There, on the platform, was the very person.

23

"Hello, Edward, you look upset," said the man.
"What's the matter, Charlie?" he asked the driver.

"There's a traction engine in the scrapyard, Vicar. He'll be broken up next week. Jem Cole says that he never drove a better engine."

"Do save him, sir. He saws wood and gives children rides," Edward explained.

"We'll see," said the Vicar.

Jem Cole came on Saturday.

"The Reverend is coming to see you, Trevor. Maybe he'll buy you."

"Do you think he will?" asked Trevor hopefully.

"He will when I've lit your fire and cleaned you up," said Jem.

The Vicar and his two boys arrived that evening. Trevor hadn't felt so happy for months. He chuffered about the yard, his green paint gleaming.

"Show what you can do, Trevor," said the Vicar.

A little while later the Vicar came out of the scrapyard office smiling.

"I've got him cheap, Jem, cheap," he said.

Jem was extremely pleased and ran to tell Trevor the good news.

"Do you hear that, Trevor?" cried Jem. "The Reverend has saved you. He is taking you to live at the vicarage with him. There is a huge orchard with a shed in it, which will be perfect for you."

"Peep, peep!" whistled Trevor happily.

Now Trevor's home is in the vicarage orchard and he sees Edward every day. His paint is spotless and his brass shines like gold.

Trevor likes his work, but his happiest day is the Church Fête. Then, with a wooden seat bolted to his bunker, he chuffers round the orchard giving rides to all the little children.

Long afterwards you will see him shut his eyes – remembering.

"I like children," he whispers happily to himself.

Thomas and Trevor

Trevor the Traction Engine enjoys living in the vicarage orchard on the Island of Sodor. Edward the Blue Engine once helped to save him from being turned into scrap, so now Trevor lives at the vicarage and the two engines are great friends.

Edward comes to see Trevor every day. Sometimes Trevor is sad because he doesn't have enough work to do.

"I do like to keep busy all the time," Trevor sighed one day, "and I do like company, especially children's company."

"Cheer up," smiled Edward. "The Fat Controller has work for you at his new harbour – I'm to take you to meet Thomas today."

"Oh!" exclaimed Trevor happily. "A harbour, the seaside, children, that will be lovely."

Trevor's truck was coupled behind Edward and they set off to meet Thomas.

Thomas was making his way to the harbour with a trainload of metal pilings. They were needed to make the harbour wall firm and safe.

"Hello, Thomas," said Edward. "This is Trevor, a friend of mine. He's a Traction Engine."

Thomas eyed the newcomer doubtfully. "A *what* engine?" he asked.

"A Traction Engine," explained Trevor. "I run on roads instead of rails. Can you take me to the harbour, please? The Fat Controller has a job for me."

"Of course," replied Thomas. But he was still puzzled.

Workmen coupled Trevor's truck to Thomas's train and soon they were ready to start their journey.

"I'm glad the Fat Controller needs me," called Trevor. "I don't have enough to do sometimes, you know, although I can work anywhere – in orchards, on farms, in scrapyards, even at harbours."

"But you don't run on rails," puffed Thomas.

"I'm a Traction Engine – I don't need rails to be useful," replied Trevor. "You wait and see."

When they reached the harbour they found everything in confusion. Trucks had been derailed, blocking the line, and stone slabs lay everywhere.

"We must get these pilings through," said Thomas's driver. "They are essential. Trevor," he said, "we need you to drag them round this mess."

"Exactly the sort of job I like," replied Trevor happily.

"Now you'll see, Thomas – I'll soon show you what Traction Engines can do."

Trevor was as good as his word. First he dragged the stones clear with chains. Then he towed the pilings into position.

"Who needs rails?" he muttered cheerfully to himself.

Later Thomas brought his two coaches, Annie and Clarabel, to visit Trevor.

Thomas was most impressed.

"Now I understand how useful a Traction Engine can be," he said.

Thomas's coaches were full of children and Trevor gave them rides along the harbour. Of all the jobs he did at the harbour that day, he liked this best of all.

"He's very kind," Annie remarked.

"He reminds me of Thomas," added Clarabel.

Everyone was sorry when it was time for Trevor to go. Thomas pulled him along the line to the junction.

A small tear came into Trevor's eye. Thomas pretended not to see and whistled gaily to try to make Trevor feel happy.

"I'll come and see you as often as I can," Thomas promised. "The Vicar will look after you, and there's plenty of work for you now at the orchard, but we may need you again at the harbour some day."

"That would be wonderful," said Trevor happily.

That evening, Trevor stood in the orchard remembering his new friend, Thomas, the harbour and most of all – the children. Then he went happily to sleep in the shed at the bottom of the orchard.

Duck Takes Charge

"Do you know what?" asked Percy.

"What?" grunted Gordon.

"Do you know what?"

"Silly," said Gordon, crossly, "of course I don't know what, if you don't tell me what what is."

"The Fat Controller says that the work in the yard is too heavy for me," said Percy. "He's getting a bigger engine to help me."

"Rubbish!" said James. "Any engine could do it," he went on grandly. "If you worked more and chattered less this yard would be a sweeter, a better, and a happier place."

Percy went off to fetch some coaches.

"That stupid old signal," he thought. He was remembering the time when

he had misunderstood a signal and gone backwards instead of forwards.

"No one listens to me now. They think I'm a silly little engine, and order me about. I'll show them! I'll show them!" he puffed as he ran about the yard. But he didn't know how. By the end of the afternoon he felt tired and unhappy.

He brought some of the coaches to the station and stood puffing at the side of the platform.

"Hello, Percy!" said the Fat Controller. "You look tired."

"Yes, sir, I am, sir," said Percy. "I don't know if I'm standing on my dome or on my wheels."

"You look the right way up to me," laughed the Fat Controller. "Cheer up! The new engine is bigger than you, and can probably do the work alone."

"Would you like to help build my new harbour? Thomas and Toby are helping."

"Oh yes, sir. Thank you, sir," said Percy happily.

The new engine arrived next morning.

"What's your name?" asked the Fat Controller kindly.

"Montague, sir. But I'm usually called 'Duck'," he replied. "They say I waddle." The engine smiled. "I don't really, sir, but I like 'Duck' better than Montague."

"Good!" said the Fat Controller. "Duck it shall be. Here Percy, show Duck round."

The two engines went off together. Soon they were busy.

James, Gordon and Henry watched Duck quietly and efficiently doing his work.

"He seems a simple sort of engine," they whispered. "We'll have some fun and order him about."

"Quaa-aa-aak! Quaa-aa-aak!" they wheezed whenever they passed him.

Smoke billowed everywhere.

Percy was cross, but Duck took no notice.

"They'll get tired of it soon," he said. "Do they tell you to do things, Percy?"

"Yes they do!" answered Percy, frowning crossly.

"Right," said Duck, "we'll soon stop *that* nonsense."

He whispered something to Percy and then said, "We'll do it later."

The Fat Controller had had a good day. He was looking forward to hot buttered toast for tea at home. All of a sudden he heard a most extraordinary noise. "Bother!" he said, looking out of the window. He hurried to the yard.

Henry, Gordon and James were "wheeshing" and snorting furiously while Duck and Percy sat calmly on the points outside the shed, refusing to let the other engines in.

"STOP THAT NOISE," bellowed the Fat Controller.

"They won't let us in," hissed the big engines.

"Duck! Explain this behaviour," demanded the Fat Controller.

"Beg pardon, sir, but I'm a Great Western Engine. We do our work without fuss. But begging your pardon sir, Percy and I would be glad if you would inform these – er – engines that we only take orders from you."

The big engines blew their whistles loudly.

"SILENCE!" snapped the Fat Controller.

"Percy and Duck," he said, "I'm pleased with your work today; but *not* with your behaviour tonight. You have caused a disturbance."

Percy and Duck started to look very worried.

Gordon, Henry and James sniggered.

"As for you," thundered the Fat Controller, "you've been worse. You made the disturbance! Duck is quite right. This is my railway and I give the orders."

Later Percy went away and Duck was left to manage alone. And he did so . . . easily!

Pop Goes The Diesel

Duck is very proud of being Great Western. He talks endlessly about it. But he works hard too and makes everything go like clockwork.

Today it was a splendid day on the Island of Sodor. The trucks and coaches were behaving well, and the passengers had stopped grumbling! But the engines didn't like having to bustle about.

"There are two ways of doing things," Duck told them. "The Great Western way, or the wrong way. I'm Great Western and . . ."

"Don't we know it," the engines groaned.

James, Gordon and Henry were glad when a visitor came. He purred smoothly towards them.

The Fat Controller introduced him. "Here is Diesel," he said. "I have agreed to give him a trial. He needs to learn. Please teach him, Duck."

"Good morning," purred Diesel in an oily voice. "Pleased to meet you, Duck. Is that James – *and* Henry – *and* Gordon, too? I am delighted to meet such famous engines."

The silly engines were flattered.

"He has very good manners," they murmured to each other. "We are very pleased to have him in our yard."

Duck had his doubts. "Come on," he said, impatiently.

"Ah yes!" said Diesel. "The yard, of course. Excuse me, engines."

Diesel purred after Duck, talking hard. "Your worthy Fat . . ."

"Sir Topham Hatt to you," ordered Duck.

Diesel looked hurt. "Your worthy Sir Topham Hatt thinks I need to learn. He is mistaken. We diesels don't need to learn. We know everything. We come to a yard and improve it. We are revolutionary."

"Oh!" said Duck. "If you're so revo–thingummy, perhaps you would collect my trucks while I fetch Gordon's coaches."

Diesel, delighted to show off, purred away.

When Duck returned, Diesel was trying to take some trucks from a siding. They were old and empty, and had not been used for a long time. Diesel found them extremely hard to move.

Pull – push – backwards – forwards.

"Oheeer! Oheeer!" the trucks groaned. "We can't! We won't!"

Duck watched with interest.

Diesel lost patience. "GrrRRRrrrRRR!" he roared, and gave a great heave. The trucks jerked forward.

"Oh! Oh!" they screamed. "We can't! We *won't*!" Some of their brakes snapped and the gear jammed in the sleepers.

"GrrRRRrrrRRR!" roared Diesel.

"Ho! Ho! Ho!" chuckled Duck.

Diesel recovered and tried to push the trucks back, but they wouldn't move an inch.

Duck ran quietly round to collect the other trucks. "Thank you for arranging these, Diesel," he said. "I must go now."

"Don't you want this lot?" asked Diesel.

"No, thank you," replied Duck.

Diesel gulped. "And I've taken all this trouble," he almost shrieked. "Why didn't you tell me?"

"You never asked me. Besides," said Duck, innocently, "you were having such a lot of fun being revo-whatever-it-was-you-said. Goodbye."

Diesel had to help the workmen clear up. He hated it. All the trucks were laughing and singing at him.

"Trucks are waiting in the yard;
tackling them with ease'll
'Show the world what I can do,'
gaily boasts the diesel.
In and out he creeps about,
like a big black weasel.
When he pulls the wrong trucks out
– Pop goes the Diesel!"

The song grew louder and louder and soon it echoed through the yard.

"Grrr!" growled Diesel and scuttled away to sulk in the shed.

When Duck returned, and heard the trucks singing, he was horrified. "Shut up!" he ordered and bumped them hard.

"I'm sorry our trucks were rude to you, Diesel," he said.

Diesel was still furious. "It's all your fault. You made them laugh at me."

"Nonsense," said Henry, "Duck would never do that. We engines have our differences; but we *never* talk about them to the trucks. That would be des – des . . ."

"Disgraceful!" said Gordon.

"Disgusting!" put in James.

"Despicable!" finished Henry.

Diesel hated Duck. He wanted him to be sent away. So he made a plan. He was going to tell lies about Duck.

Next day he spoke to the trucks. "I see you like jokes. You made a good joke about me yesterday. I laughed and laughed. Duck told me one about Gordon. I'll whisper it . . . don't tell Gordon I told you," said Diesel and he sniggered away.

"Haw! Haw! Haw!" guffawed the trucks. "Gordon will be cross with Duck when he knows. Let's tell him and pay Duck back for bumping us."

They laughed rudely at the engines as they went by. Soon Gordon, Henry and James found out why.

"Disgraceful!" said Gordon.

"Disgusting!" said James.

"Despicable!" said Henry. "We cannot allow it."

They consulted together. "Yes," they said, "he did it to us. We'll do it to him, and see how *he* likes it."

Duck was tired. The trucks had been cheeky and troublesome. He wanted a rest in the shed.

But the engines barred his way.

"Hooooosh! KEEP OUT!" they hissed.

"Stop fooling," said Duck, "I'm tired."

"So are we," said the engines. "We are tired of *you*. We like Diesel. We don't like you. You tell tales about us to the trucks."

"I don't."

"You do."

"I don't."

"You do."

The Fat Controller came to stop the noise.

"Duck called me a 'galloping sausage'," spluttered Gordon.

". . . rusty old scrap iron," hissed James.

". . . I'm 'old square wheels'," fumed Henry.

"Well, Duck?" said the Fat Controller, trying not to laugh.

Duck considered. "I only wish, sir," he said gravely, "that I'd thought of those names myself. If the dome fits . . ."

"He made the trucks laugh at us," said the engines.

"Did you, Duck?" asked the Fat Controller.

"Certainly not, sir. No *steam* engine would be as mean as that."

Diesel lurked up.

"Now, Diesel, you heard what Duck said," said the Fat Controller.

"I can't understand it, sir," said Diesel. "To think that Duck of all engines . . . I'm dreadfully grieved, sir, but I know nothing."

"I see," said the Fat Controller.

Diesel squirmed and hoped he didn't.

"I'm sorry, Duck," said the Fat Controller, "but you must go to Edward's station for a while. I know he will be glad to see you."

"As you wish, sir," said Duck, and he trundled sadly away, while Diesel smirked with triumph.

A Close Shave

Duck the Great Western Engine puffed sadly into Edward's station.

"It's not fair," he complained. "Diesel has been telling lies about me and made the Fat Controller and all the engines think I'm horrid. They think I told tales about them to the trucks and now the Fat Controller has sent me away."

Edward smiled. "I know you aren't horrid," he said, "and so does the Fat Controller, you wait and see. Would you help me with these trucks?"

Duck felt happier with Edward. He set to work at once and helped Edward with his trucks and coaches.

The trucks were silly, heavy and noisy. The two engines had to work hard pushing and pulling all afternoon. At last they reached the top of the hill.

"Peep, peep! Goodbye," whistled Duck, and rolled gently over the crossing to the other line.

Duck loved coasting down the hill, running easily with the wind whistling past. He hummed a little tune. Suddenly he heard a whistling sound. "Peeeeep! Peeeeep!"

"That sounds like a guard's whistle," he thought. "But we haven't a guard." His driver heard it too, and looked back.

"Hurry, Duck, hurry!" he called urgently.

"There's been a breakaway and some trucks are chasing us."

"Hurrah! Hurrah! Hurrah!" laughed the trucks. "We've broken away! We've broken away! We've broken away!"

And before the signalman could change the points they followed Duck on down the line.

"Chase him, bump him, throw him off the rails," they yelled and hurtled after Duck, bumping and swaying with ever increasing speed.

Duck raced through Edward's station, whistling furiously, but the trucks were catching up.

"As fast as we can," said the driver. "Then they'll catch us gradually." The driver was gaining control. "Another clear mile and we'll do it," he said. "Oh glory! Look at that!"

James was just pulling out on their line from the station ahead.

Any minute now there could be a crash!

"It's up to you now, Duck," cried the driver.

Duck put every ounce of weight and steam against the trucks. They felt his strength. "On! On!" they yelled.

"I must stop them. I *must*," cried Duck. The station came nearer and nearer. The last coach cleared the platform.

"It's too late!" Duck whistled. He felt a sudden swerve, and slid shuddering and groaning along a siding.

A barber had set up shop in a wooden shed in the siding. He was shaving a customer. There was a sliding, groaning crash, and part of the wall caved in.

The silly trucks had knocked their guard off his van and left him far behind after he had whistled a warning.

But the trucks didn't care – they were feeling very pleased with themselves.

"Beg pardon, sir!" gasped Duck.

"Please excuse my intrusion."

"No, I won't!" said the barber, crossly. "Not only have you frightened my customers but you've spoilt my new paint too. I'll teach you." And with that he lathered Duck's face all over. Poor Duck.

Thomas was helping to pull the trucks away when the Fat Controller arrived. The barber was telling the workmen what he thought.

"I do not like engines popping through my walls," he fumed. "They disturb my customers."

"I appreciate your feelings," said the Fat Controller, "and we'll gladly repair the damage. But you must know that this engine and his crew have prevented a serious accident. You and many others might have been badly hurt."

The Fat Controller paused impressively.

"It was a very close shave!" he said.

"Oh!" said the barber. "Excuse me." He filled a basin of water to wash Duck's face. "I'm sorry," he said. "I didn't know you were being a brave engine."

48

"That's all right sir," said Duck. "I didn't know that either."

"You were very brave indeed," said the Fat Controller, kindly. "I'm very proud of you."

"Oh, sir!" sighed Duck. He felt happier than he had done for weeks.

The Fat Controller watched the rescue operation. "And when you are properly washed and mended," he said to Duck, "you are coming home."

"Home, sir?" asked Duck. "Do you mean the yard?"

"Of course," said the Fat Controller.

"But sir, they don't like me. They like Diesel," said Duck sadly.

"Not now." The Fat Controller smiled. "I never believed Diesel," he said, "so I sent him packing. The engines are sorry and want you back."

A few days later, when he came home, there was a really rousing welcome for Duck the Great Western Engine.

Thomas Comes To Breakfast

Thomas the Tank Engine has worked his branch line for many years, and knows it very well.

"You know just where to stop, Thomas," laughed his driver. "You could almost manage it without me!"

Thomas had become conceited. He didn't realise that his driver was joking.

Later he boasted to the others. "Driver says I don't need him now."

"Don't be daft," snorted Percy. "An engine can't go without its driver."

"I'd never go without *my* driver," said Toby earnestly. "I'd be too frightened."

"Pooh!" boasted Thomas. "I'm not scared."

"You'd never dare," said the other engines.

"I would then," boasted Thomas. "You'll see!"

Next morning the fireman came. Thomas drowsed comfortably in the shed as the warmth spread through his boiler. Percy and Toby were still asleep. Thomas opened his eyes and then he suddenly remembered. "Silly old stick in the muds," he chuckled.

"I'll show them! Driver hasn't come yet, so here goes."

He cautiously tried one piston; then the other. "They're moving! They're moving!" he whispered. "I'll just go out, then I'll stop and 'wheeesh'. That'll make them jump!"

Very, very quietly he headed past the door.

Thomas thought that he was being clever, but really he was only moving because a careless cleaner had meddled with his controls. He soon found out his mistake.

He tried to "wheeesh" but he couldn't. He tried to stop but he couldn't do that either. He just kept rolling along.

"The buffers will stop me!" he thought, but the siding had no buffers.

Thomas's wheels left the rails and crunched the tarmac. There was the station master's house! Thomas didn't dare to look at what was coming next. The station master and his family were sitting at the table, about to have breakfast.

"Horrors!" cried Thomas and shut his eyes tightly.

There was a crash! The house rocked and broken glass tinkled. Plaster peppered the plates.

Thomas had collected a bush on his travels. He peered anxiously into the room through its leaves. He couldn't speak. The station master was furious.

The station master's wife picked up her plate. "You miserable engine," she scolded. "Just look what you've done to our breakfast! Now I shall have to cook some more."

She banged the door. More plaster fell. This time, it fell on Thomas.

Thomas felt depressed. The plaster was tickly. He wanted to sneeze but he didn't dare in case the house fell on him. Nobody came for a long time. Everyone was much too busy.

At last workmen propped up the house with strong poles and laid rails through the garden.

Donald and Douglas arrived.

"Dinna fash yerself, Thomas. We'll soon hae ye back on the rails," they laughed.

Puffing hard, the twins managed to haul Thomas back to safety.

Bits of fencing, the bush and a broken window frame festooned Thomas's front, which was badly twisted. He looked very funny.

The twins laughed and left him.

Thomas was in disgrace, but there was worse to come.

"You are a very naughty engine," came a voice.

"I know, sir," said Thomas. "I'm sorry, sir." Thomas's voice was muffled behind his bush.

"You must go to the works and have your front end mended. It will be a long job," said the Fat Controller.

"Yes, sir," faltered Thomas.

"Meanwhile, a diesel railcar called Daisy will do your work."

"A d-d-diesel, sir? D-D-Daisy, sir?" Thomas spluttered.

"Yes, Thomas," said the Fat Controller. "Diesels *always* stay in their sheds till they are wanted. Diesels *never* gallivant off to breakfast in station masters' houses."

The Fat Controller turned on his heels, and sternly walked away.

Percy and Harold

Percy worked hard at the new harbour. The men needed stone for their building work. Toby helped, but sometimes the loads of stone were too heavy and Percy had to fetch them for himself.

Sometimes, as he pulled the trucks along the harbour quay, Percy would see Thomas.

"Well done, Percy," Thomas would say. "The Fat Controller is very pleased with us."

There was an airfield close to the harbour. Percy heard the aeroplanes zooming overhead all day. The noisiest of all was a helicopter which hovered overhead, buzzing like an angry bee.

"Stupid thing!" Percy would say, as he ran past the airfield. "Why can't it go and buzz somewhere else?"

One day Percy stopped at the airfield. The helicopter was standing quite close.

"Hello!" said Percy. "Who are you?"

"I'm Harold," said the helicopter. "Who are you?"

"I'm Percy. What whirly great arms you've got."

"They're nice arms," said Harold. "I can hover like a bird. Don't you wish you could hover?"

"Certainly not!" said Percy. "I like my rails, thank you."

"I think railways are slow," said Harold. "They're not much use and quite out of date."

Harold whirled his arms and buzzed away.

Percy angrily puffed off to find Toby who was working at the quarry.

"I say, Toby," he burst out, "that Harold, that stuck-up whirlibird thing, says I'm slow and out of date. Just let him wait, I'll show him."

Percy collected his trucks and started off, still fuming.

Soon, above the clatter of the trucks, he heard a familiar buzzing.

"Percy," whispered his driver, "there's Harold. He's not far ahead. Let's race him."

"Yes, let's," said Percy excitedly and, quickly gathering speed, he steamed off down the line.

Percy pounded along, and the trucks screamed and swayed as they gathered speed together on their journey through the valley.

"Well, I'll be a ding-a-dong-danged!" said the driver. There was Harold, high above them – the race was on!

"Go on, Percy!" yelled his driver. "You're gaining."

Percy had never been allowed to run fast before; he was having the time of his life!

"Hurry! Hurry! Hurry!" he panted to the trucks.

"We don't want to, we don't want to," they grumbled.

But it was no use; Percy was bucketing along with flying wheels, and Harold was high above, alongside him.

The fireman shovelled for dear life while Percy's driver leaned out of the cab and cheered Percy along.

He was so excited he could hardly keep still.

"Well done, Percy," he shouted. "We're gaining! We're going ahead! Oh good boy, good boy!"

Far ahead, a distant signal warned them that the harbour wharf was near.

"Peep, peep, peep," whistled Percy, as he approached the wharf. "Brakes, guard, please!" he said.

The driver carefully checked the train's headlong speed. They rolled under the main line, and halted on the wharf.

"Oh dear!" groaned Percy, "I'm sure we've lost."

The fireman scrambled to the cab roof.

"We've won! We've won!" he shouted. "Harold's still hovering. He's looking for a place to land!"

"Listen boys!" he called. "Here's a song for Percy:

*Said Harold Helicopter to our Percy,
'You are slow!
Your railway is out of date and not much use you know.'
But Percy, with his stone trucks, did the trip in record time.
And we beat the helicopter on our old branch line!"*

The driver and the guard soon caught the tune and so did the workmen on the quay.

Percy loved it. "Oh, thank you!" he said. He liked the last line best of all.

Later Percy and Toby went back to the shed. Percy was a very happy engine indeed.